The Holiday Court

Hiding Destiny

5

K. M. Robinson

HIDING DESTINY

Crescent Sea
PUBLISHING

Published by Crescent Sea Publishing.
www.crescentseapublishing.com

Cover designed by Cover A Day.
www.coveraday.com

To those who do the difficult things so others don't have to.

THE HOLIDAY COURT

You can read The Holiday Court Series in any order you like! It all revolves around one catastrophic event and the daughters of the Court leaders each have to handle a different problem to save their people from the same villain so you'll get a different character's perspective in each story!

Here's who you'll meet:

Saving North (Christmas)
Reviving Time (New Years)
Targeting Bliss (Valentine's Day)
Pressing Luck (St Patrick's Day)
Hiding Destiny (Easter)
Tricking Fate (Halloween)

CHAPTER 1

"This room is off-limits, mistress." The deep voice frightened Evangeline, making her jump.

Slamming the book shut while careful to keep her finger between the pages to mark her place, she looked up to find a Winter Guard peering down at her. His uniform was pristine—it reminded Evangeline of a nutcracker doll.

“You know Jubilee’s father has given me permission to be here,” Evangeline countered, annoyed.

“There’s a party, ma’am, you should be there,” Asher replied cooly.

“My attendance is not required anywhere.” Evangeline turned back to her book, opening it again.

The lights in the library were dim enough that people wandering the hallways of the Winter Palace wouldn’t take notice. It gave her just enough light to read by, though it tinged the pages of the perfectly preserved book a deep yellow, making her eyes strain slightly.

"Your father might beg to differ."

“Which is why I asked Santa and not my father.” She didn’t bother to look up.

“I do not have time to guard a *princess* tonight,” Asher said, stepping closer. “I have enough to do, and a stray partygoer isn’t on the list of things to monitor.

“Then don’t.”

“Excuse me?” Asher’s reply was indignant. He stepped closer again, this time putting his hand on the table in front of the egg painter’s daughter. “Just because your father is the most renowned artist in all the kingdoms doesn’t mean you get to throw your weight around. This room is off limits because we have thousands of people, elves, and fae in attendance tonight and we need to keep everyone safe. You being in this room causes a problem for us because we have far too much to oversee as it is. Now get up and walk out of here on your own, princess, or I will pick you up and carry you back to the gala.”

“You wouldn’t dare!” Evangeline whipped her eyes up to look at him. The look she found told her the Winter Guard was deadly serious.

“I’ve told you before and I’ll tell you again, guard, I do not wish to speak with you,” she retorted hoping he’d let her sit quietly.

Though Evangeline was friends with the Holiday Court leader's daughters, she preferred small group settings. Spending time with the girls was one thing but being subjected to a massive, multi-room gala where everyone had a love interest or boyfriend was not her idea of a good time. She'd much rather hide away in the library studying the manuscripts and histories Santa held onto for the court leaders.

"And Jubilee Claus has told you to trust and listen to me, and I'm telling you it's time to go—"

His words were cut off by a voice in the hallway.

"No one is supposed to be in this wing," Asher grumbled quietly under his breath. He stepped forward, preparing to remove the trespassers but froze when Father Time came into view—the court leaders didn't have to adhere to the same restrictions as everyone else.

Asher rocked back on his feet, settling in next to Evangeline. She thought about calling out to Father Time to get further permission to be in the library instead of at the party, but she knew getting Asher in trouble would only lead to him giving her more grief down the road. They had a turbulent history at best.

The doors to the library were massively wide when opened all of the way. This evening, they were stretched open to give the guards easy access to make sure no one had slipped off for a stolen moment from the party.

It took a painfully long time for Father Time and the men he was with to cross the illuminated space. It was hard to see their features with the backlighting.

"Darkness is right though." Father Time's voice drifted to them softly. "This needs to be done."

"Darkness?" Asher whispered, leaning forward again.

Evangeline sat up in the chair, suddenly aware that if they could see Father Time, they could also be spotted, even if the lighting was dimmed in the room. Quietly, she removed her finger from the volume she had been reading, knowing that time was over.

"He sent specific instructions for you, Father Time," the man next to him said, handing him a piece of paper. "Once you've handled everyone tonight, he'll be waiting for you at the palace..."

They disappeared from sight. Without waiting, Asher rushed to the door as their voices faded away. Evangeline stood up, following him quickly. They paused at the door, looking around carefully as Evangeline held back her dark hair out of the way.

"I hope you'll remember me when this is all finished, Father Time," the man—no, elf—next to him continued. "I was instrumental in this takeover. You wouldn't be able to capture the leaders if it hadn't been for my work."

Evangeline's heart jumped into her throat—Father Time was working with Darkness to overtake the Court.

Her best friend's father was working against them. Asher tensed next to her as he watched them walk down the marble-covered hall.

"You will not be forgotten." Father Time was interrupted as more elves joined him dressed for the gala.

"It's a coup," Asher said, voice dropping in disbelief. "Father Time is betraying us."

Her mind raced as she tried to reconcile what was happening. Father Time had always been strict on Viv since she was to take over after him, but she never thought he'd betray them all—he seemed too close to Santa and the others.

Asher turned to Evangeline. "Stay here."

She latched onto his arm, digging her nails into his muscles to hold him in place. "Where do you think you're going?"

"I have to stop them," he insisted.

"There's one of you and seven of them," she pointed out harshly. "If you go running in there like the hero you think you are, they'll subdue you and I'll be left here to get word to the others about what is happening. Do you honestly think I can get by seven full-grown men on a mission to warn Santa and the others that Father Time has decided to work with Darkness and the rebel elves?"

Every muscle in Asher's face was tightened, nostrils flaring. His ears were pressed back against his head as his jutted jaw pulled back the skin near his temples and ears. Realizing her point, he relaxed his jaw, smoothing out the harshness across his face.

"You and I have to warn the others and *then* we can stop whatever is happening here," Evangeline continued, tucking her hair back over her shoulder.

"You heard it though, right? They're planning an overthrow." His hazel eyes flashed with anger, for once not directed at her.

"I heard it. We need to find the leaders."

"We don't know who else might be involved in this—we need to be careful. I'm certain Santa is not—we need to locate him and warn him."

Asher worked closely enough with Santa to know if something had changed. Evangeline couldn't imagine the other court leaders betraying everyone to work with Darkness, but she also hadn't imagined her friend's father planning a coup either—though if anyone would, it would be Viv's dad.

"Come this way, there's a secret passage we can use to circumnavigate them." Asher waved her forward.

Hurrying behind him, Evangeline kept close. She might not like the Winter Guard, but she deferred to him on this matter. Jubilee was her most trusted friend and she spoke highly of the guard much more often than Evangeline would like.

The hallways of the Winter Palace were covered in marble floors and magnificent tapestries. Brushing one of the wall hangings aside, Asher revealed a hidden door.

Inside the passageway, lights glowed a dark yellow, reminding Evangeline of the library she had just vacated. She had planned an evening of literature and histories, with a few moments of time with her friends later in the evening. Making her heart pound in secret hallways was not her idea of a good time.

"We'll go to the center, it will be easiest to find someone to help there, even if it's the other guards," Asher said, reaching up to move his blond bangs out of his eyes. The movement made him look slightly less pristine, almost humanizing him.

“We need to find Viv and see what she knows about her father’s plan.”

“She’s not involved,” Asher assured her.

“Of course not!” Evangeline chastised him, snapping. “Why would you even suggest such a thing?”

“I’m telling you I know her well enough to know she has nothing to do with this—I’m trying to show you I’m on your side.” Asher’s protest was sharp as he whipped his head over his shoulder to glare at her. “You have to twist everything into some injury against you, don’t you?”

“I do no such thing!” Evangeline’s blood boiled, sending heat up and down her forearms as Asher picked up the pace to force her to move faster than she was comfortable.

"Sure, princess, you've *never* done that before."

"I don't twist your words," she protested, arms pumping quickly to run behind him as he sprinted.

"No, you just take everything as an insult. Even when I tried being nice to you, you were against me."

"You never tried to be nice to me, *guard*." Evangeline's insults were lacking, but it was the best she could do at the moment.

"I'll always be just a guard to you..." Asher grumbled. "At least the others see me as a person....an equal."

"Then I guess it's a good thing you spend time with Jubilee, Viv, and Libi, and not me," Evangeline snipped back.

Asher turned on his heels to the right, moving three more steps before slamming to a halt. Evangeline crashed into him, pushing him against the closed door.

"Watch it," he chided.

"How was I supposed to know there was a door here?" Indignant, Evangeline reached down to smooth out her black dress.

Turning, Asher looked her up and down slowly. Reaching up, he dropped a hand in her hair, deliberately dragging it down her long locks.

"You have flower petals in your hair." He said quietly,

dragging out his words as slowly as his hand moving down the side of her face, tangling in her hair.

Evangeline's lips parted in shock. His fingers gently moved the strands of her hair reminding her of when her father used to brush it out for her when she was a child. She blinked trying to maintain her composure.

Her breath caught in the back of her mouth just above her throat and she swallowed hard to try to trigger herself into thinking straight again.

Reaching up, she knocked his hand back.

"How dare you!"

"How dare I what? How dare I try to help you look presentable before we walk out in public? What would people think if they saw us stepping out of the secret hallways looking like we just ran off from the party together?"

"*Like I would sneak off from a party with you*," she muttered.

"That's right," he said, tipping his head flirtatiously to the side, "you only sneak off for books."

"When have you ever met a person that's more interesting than the contents of the books in that library?" Evangeline countered.

"You need to get out more, princess." He shook his head, turning back to open the door. "For example, a party. You clearly made it into the Easter room long enough to be showered in flower petals...why didn't you stay and try to meet some people?"

"I know all the people I need to know." Evangeline crossed her arms as Asher checked to make sure the hall was clear before stepping out.

"Well, at least you know you can trust me, even if you don't like me." He stepped out of the passageway, clearly upset. "Now, come on, we're here."

Chapter 2

The hallway was as quiet as the passageway had been. Voices sounded from around the corner—the court leaders' daughters were already gathering, as Evangeline knew they would.

The voices were hushed but Evangeline could make them out. She picked up Jubilee's voice first.

"Adaire and I arrested the elven intruders this evening but apparently it was part of their plot to get into the Pole during the gala," Santa's daughter said.

"What's the plan?" Libi—Cupid's daughter—asked.

"We need to rescue the leaders." The man's voice sounded familiar, but Evangeline couldn't place it. Rounding the corner, she spotted an incredibly handsome fae prince standing next to Father Time's Daughter, Viv—Prince Eliad. "We'll split up—keep the parties away from the fighting but warn the guards at each to be prepared—the enemy doesn't need to know we're coming. We stand our best chance if we don't alert them that we know what's happening."

"We'll find out what they want." Jubilee stared at the fae prince next to Viv.

"We know what they want." Evangeline took that as her cue. Asher moved quickly behind her, heat radiating off of him. "I was in one of the studies and overheard part of their plan. Your father is working with Darkness, Viv—Father Time is controlling this attack."

"*Why*?" Tempest clenched her jaw, fingers tightening into a ball.

"*He was serious*?" Libi dragged her attention back to Viv as she mumbled under her breath—Viv's father must have done something else recently that she hadn't shared with everyone yet.

"Serious about what?" Evangeline tugged at the bow on her black dress sleeve, anxiety filling her body.

"I can't believe he would... No." Viv looked at various spots on the marble floor. Evangeline waited, giving Libi room to guide the conversation—she was the best at facilitating deep discussions and getting to the heart of it quickly. Evangeline would have jumped in too quickly and made it worse, so it was better to be silent and wait.

"Viv, what is it?" Libi asked in a soft voice. The fae prince next to Viv looked to Libi, dragging his eyes away from Father Time's daughter.

Glancing around the group, Evangeline saw the tension in Jubilee's body. Next to her, Prince Adaire of the refugee elves at the North Pole mimicked her stressed appearance. She was glad he was there to stop his former subjects from taking over the Pole—after all, it was his responsibility to help with this. Santa has been gracious enough to allow them into the North Pole, now it was time to repay the favor and help protect it.

Tempest stood next to Jubilee dressed in a slightly-less-lavish-than-usual dress. It surprised Evangeline to see her in a more subdued dress, but that only meant Tempest must have an extravagant mask she had taken off at some point—the queen of Halloween wouldn't be caught in anything less than glamourous.

"He said he wanted to stop time. He said it over and over." Viv's voice was sad.

"Why?" Ridge—Tempest's ex-boyfriend—asked, stepping into the circle.

"He said he didn't trust me to run time," Viv announced.

"He's seriously pulling the party girl card again?" Tempest asked.

"We have to stop Father Time," Jubilee redirected them. "If the New Year doesn't happen, none of us can move forward—there will be no more joy, no more hope, and no more holidays. We'll all be stuck here forever."

"If we exist at all—who knows what will happen to

us," Tempest reminded them that their fate wasn't certain if Father Time and Darkness' plan was realized.

"That only gives us an hour—the Year changes soon," Libi said.

"How would your father do this, Viv?" Jubilee asked.

"I'm not sure, he's been talking about how time moves forward recently." Viv paused to think as her new fae prince put his hand on her elbow and rubbed it. Evangeline cringed, partly out of disgust for a man being so intimate with her friend that she had clearly just met, partly out of jealousy.

"Wait, he can't be doing this alone, can he?" Tempest asked. "He couldn't have possibly staged the attack by himself."

"You don't think he's talking to Darkness, do you?" Evangeline leading them. She brushed her hair back. "Could they be in this together?"

"Until a few moments ago, we assumed it was Darkness because he controls the rebels," Jubilee reminded them. "We wouldn't know anything if Evangeline hadn't heard Father Time."

The look on Viv's face hurt Evangeline's heart. Her friend had been through so much over the last few years, especially under the weight of her father's expectations.

"He's definitely working with Darkness—he seems like a puppet. Sorry, Viv." Evangeline said, no longer trying to get them to figure it out on their own.

"Ciara?" Libi interrupted, looking around them. "Is that you?"

A girl with red hair stepped into the room. Evangeline instantly recognized the man beside her—Cillian. He dragged an angry elf beside him, holding tightly to his collar so he couldn't escape.

Adaire clearly knew the elf—a former subject of his. Cillian refused to lessen his grip as he moved them forward.

"We found him sneaking around the halls." Cillian's voice was low and harsh. "I take it you want to speak with him?"

He nodded to Jubilee, recognizing her authority since they were in her kingdom.

"Thank you, Cillian. We do." She nodded, giving herself the authority over the situation. The captive elf didn't like that.

"You're out of time." The elf jerked forward, hissing at her. "You have no more power than former Prince Adaire did when we found our way free. You won't win this battle, Mistress Claus—yes, we know who you are."

"*Everyone* knows who I am. You haven't figured anything special out." Jubilee feigned disinterest, strengthening her power. She was strategic about her movements—Evangeline approved.

"Oh, but we have, and you'll pay the price for it!" The elf lunged toward her, but Asher rushed up next to them, decisively taking action. He had always been one to process things quickly, make a decision, and act on it. Sadly, Evangeline realized they were the same in that respect.

"At your service, Mistress." Asher nodded his head to Jubilee. Technically speaking, she was as much his boss as her father was, though they had a mutual respect for each other. While not quite friends, they were close enough that they could be if they hadn't kept the lines clearly in place during work hours.

"Excellent timing, Asher," Jubilee praised him. They had developed a rapport over the years of his service in the Winter Palace.

The blond guard dug his nails into the elf's shoulder, making him cry out in pain. "Oh, *you'll talk*," Asher mumbled attractively under his breath. Evangeline gulped, catching herself.

"We can't wait around for him to tell us everything," Tempest interjected, annoyed.

Asher dragged the traitor back, slamming him against the wall. He leaned in closely and murmured threats, giving the others space to speak without being overheard. Evangeline turned away from him.

"What do you know, Ciara?" Libi asked quietly, returning her attention to the group. Jubilee opened her mouth to speak but Libi glared, forbidding her from talking over the redhead.

"We were in the hallway before we found the rebel," Cillian answered for her gently—Ciara clearly didn't like being put on the spot and Evangeline couldn't blame her. "We saw where Father Time was going."

"He left?" Viv asked, her voice going quiet. Evangeline leaned in wanting to support her friend without causing a scene. "Where did he go?"

"He was headed in the direction of the Clock Tower. I'd guess he was going there. What do you think, Ciara?" He leaned closer to his girlfriend and nodded.

"I agree, it was the Clock Tower or something near it, but I also saw something else." Ciara reached up to tuck her long curls behind her shoulder. Evangeline was jealous of how long her hair was. "He sent some of the rebels out with something and told them to take care of everyone."

"What does that mean?" Tempest asked, voice dipping down in frustration.

"I can answer that one—it's a substance he uses to subdue and calm fears," Viv said, taking charge of the conversation. "So much is unknown about the future that there are individuals who can get so overwhelmed that he needs to help calm them."

"You mean he's going to control us?" Jubilee's jaw tightened, matching Evangeline's. "We need to split up."

Jubilee handed out assignments as the rest waited. Evangeline stood, annoyed, already knowing where she would be assigned. Jubilee had been trying to pair her with Asher for years and this was her chance.

"Adaire and I will stop anyone else from entering the Pole and get the rebels that are already here out," Santa's daughter announced. "We'll protect everyone in the Palace."

"We'll stop this." Adaire echoed her statement, placing a hand over his chest. Jubilee eyed him without turning to look at him...something was going on there, but Evangeline would have to ask questions later.

"I'm going after my father," Viv interrupted abruptly, drawing everyone's attention.

"Are you sure that's a good idea, Viv?" Jubilee asked, taking a small step forward. "He knows you too well—"

"I'm the one who will take his role—it has to be me. I know he is aware of how I work...but I'm also aware of how *he* works. If anyone is going to be able to predict his moves and stop him, it's me. And out of all of us, I'm the one he'll underestimate the most." No one argued with her.

"I'll assist." Viv's fae prince moved closer to her as he volunteered his service. Jubilee eyed Viv, waiting for her approval.

"Libi, can you manage to stop this mind-subduing agent?" Jubilee asked, turning to her.

"Absolutely. Orion and I can take care of that and make sure everyone in the parties are safe. I'm guessing they'll go straight to dosing the food and drink, but we'll see." Libi started to inch away. Evangeline wanted to join her.

"When you're done, join the fight outside and bring reinforcements once you're sure they can be trusted and haven't been altered by the subduing agent," Jubilee concluded.

"We'll join you as quickly as possible—you hurry there, we'll bring everything we need behind you," Libi agreed quickly.

"Temp, you're going to have to save the leaders." Jubilee turned to the costume maker's daughter.

"On it, boss." Tempest swayed to the right, kicking her stance out to accommodate the hand on her hip. She turned to glance over her shoulder at Ridge confidently. "You're with me."

"You're going to need help." Libi jumped in. "Ciara and Cillian are fantastic at causing a distraction."

Cillian accepted the assignment on their behalf. The redhead blushed next to him—Evangeline would have to ask Libi about how she knew the girl later. She kept a mental list of everyone who owed her explanations.

"We'll give you an opportunity to get in and save the leaders without being noticed—we'll draw them out. We make our own luck in these situations." His hand deftly squeezed Ciara's at his side. She nodded in agreement.

"Evangeline—" Jubilee turned to her.

"I know." Evangeline sighed. "I'm interrogating the elf."

"You're the best at getting information out of people," Jubilee insisted. Evangeline knew this assignment was more than that, but she let it slide.

"That's because she's read every manual in the entire court." Tempest's joke earned her a glare, even from Libi.

"Go with Asher and help interrogate the spy," Jubilee cut Evangeline off before she could counter. "When you're done, monitor everything from my father's workshop and help to organize the rest of us. If anyone fails, Ev, you have to take their place."

"Understood." Evangeline nodded. The other girls may be fit to fight in a battle if needed, but Evangeline was prepared for psychological warfare and was ready to use it on the captive elf.

"Go!" Adaire instructed. "We have to hurry—we don't have time to waste. Be ready at a moment's notice—have your weapons in hand and be cautious!"

CHAPTER 3

Asher shoved the elf into a chair in the library. Two of the guards he trusted stood outside of the now-closed doors. Evangeline watched from a distance as Asher tried to ascertain information first.

The elf's eyes grew narrow then wide as Asher spoke quietly to him. Asher could be terrifying when he wanted to be.

Evangeline quietly moved around the room, gathering a few things. Picking up a few books, she held them in the crook of her arm. She placed a few sheets of parchment paper on her stack and quietly added a highly decorated quill pen to her collection. Tucking three vials in the crook of her arm, she turned.

Moving back, she took a seat across the table from the elf. Asher glanced at her, doing a double-take when he noticed her supplies.

"I've been told you shouldn't mess with her," Asher

said, nodding toward Evangeline. "You would have been wise to answer me...now you have to deal with her."

He settled back onto his heels, crossing his arms as he loomed over the elf. Asher kept his eyes on the rebel, ensuring he would keep Evangeline safe.

She smoothed out a piece of paper and began to draw on it the way her father had taught her how—she had always preferred paper to fragile eggshells. Silence filled the room.

Asher held deadly still, though he clearly wanted to see what Evangeline was doing. She persisted.

"My father taught me to draw," she finally murmured. "When I was a girl, I'd hold my hand out on the table and draw on my skin with deep-colored inks. The lectures I got for wasting his precious inks were unforgettable—to this day I hesitate to ever use ink for anything even though I own my own now.

"My father never appreciated my exploration," She continued as she waved her hand over the ink to dry it. "There was a certain way for things to be done. Exploration was fine, but only within the context of what we knew worked."

She glanced up, looking at the elf for the first time since she sat. The movement made Asher flinch as he saw her from the corner of his eye—the elf didn't move, hands still resting on the table in front of him.

"You see, my father is quite renowned. My family has

a way of doing things that has propelled us into the spotlight." Evangeline placed her empty hand on the table in front of her, spreading out her fingers. "My father was very clever—he knew exactly what to do to enable him to elevate our family and rise in the kingdoms.

"I have never been required to follow in his steps, you see—I've always had my own free path—but hindering his success was prohibited."

Evangeline moved slowly as if she were going to paint her own hand. She rested the edge of her palm on her fingertips to position herself to touch the ink to the back of her hand. The elf watched, leaning forward slightly to see what she would do.

Swirling the pen just above the skin, she marked out the design in the air for a moment. He leaned in further.

Evangeline darted her hand out toward him, pinning his hand to the table by using the base of her hand against his knuckles. The tip of the pen pressed firmly against his ring finger just above the cuticle.

"Go ahead, I dare you to move," she whispered.

The elf grimaced, whimpering, but he didn't move, knowing how painful it would be if she pierced his finger. He hadn't been threatened when Asher and Cillian had caused pain before, but this was different. She had found a weak spot she could exploit—his bravado was only for show.

"I see," she murmured. "Good. We'll start there."

Evangeline tossed a look to Asher, raising an eyebrow as she grinned.

"Now, if you move...at all...during our conversation, I will put this through your finger and move on to the next. Do I make myself clear?"

The elf made a noise.

"*What?*"

"Yes," the elf barked at her.

"Good. We have some questions for you." Evangeline turned to give Asher permission to speak.

He leaned in, putting a hand on the table to brace himself. "What are they planning?"

"Answer truthfully...*I* am your lie detector," Evangeline warned him.

"I don't know all of it," the elf answered.

"You know enough," Asher responded.

"They've kidnapped the leaders. They're being held down by your cells. They drugged them to subdue their powers for a time."

"How long will it last?" Asher demanded.

The elf hesitated.

Evangeline dragged the pen tip toward the elf's knuckle, a trail of ink in its wake as she looped back down to where she had started. She pressed down enough for him to feel it at the end. It frightened the elf so badly he cried out in shock. She glanced up at him, waiting for more details.

"Hours." The elf gasped. "A few hours, maybe, just long enough for them to gain control of the palace."

"You're not telling us something..." Evangeline dragged out her words. She quickly looped the pen over his finger again in a quick motion, but this time when she reached her starting point, she pressed down deeply, forcing the metal into his flesh.

The elf screamed. Asher whipped his eyes over to her, surprised, but moved in quickly, grabbing the elf's other hand and pulling a finger back just far enough to assure the rebel that he would snap it if he didn't get answers.

"The lady thinks you're holding out on us. Are you?" Asher growled.

"It's different for everyone—we don't know how long it will last!" the elf cried.

"Who won't it last on?" Evangeline demanded. "*Who*?"

"Mother Nature!" The elf yelled. "She's stronger than the rest. It will fade from her first!"

Asher let go of the elf, but Evangeline didn't move, prepared to strike again.

"How long until she is free?"

The elf glared at him. Evangeline lifted her pen and moved it to another finger.

He relented. "It will wear off within minutes. She won't know unless she tries to use her powers though—Father Time made sure of it. He knows she won't try anything if she assumes she is powerless because the others are."

Evangeline pulled the pen up his finger leaving a dark mark. He flinched under her movement. She locked eyes with him, dipping her head to see him as she leaned forward hoping she was intimidating him.

"Do you see these?" She nodded to three vials on the table she had concealed with the edges of her books. Using her free hand, she moved them into sight. "One of these is ink like my father taught me to use. One is laced with a drug that will make you sleep. The third contains a poison."

The elf paled.

"Now, *I* know which is which. I used those books right there to teach myself about these drugs...I've been coming to this library for the last month to study poisons. I've been working on crafting them, but I haven't tested them yet. Would you like to find out if they work?"

"Is that what you've been doing in here?" Asher played along, reinforcing the terrifying picture Evangeline was painting with her words and threats.

"Ask your questions." Evangeline's voice was as low and dangerous as she could make it.

Standing, she moved around the table keeping the pen attached to the man's hand. Asher began a barrage of questions that the elf had no choice but to answer.

Evangeline knelt down next to him and moved the

pen up his hand, over his wrist to his arm where she started a detailed drawing with her ink. She created a swirled pattern up and down his skin in thick black ink. When the ink slowed, she dipped it back in a vial.

"Don't worry, it won't hurt you unless it punctures the skin." She smiled without looking up as the elf watched her. "Aren't you curious which one this is? Death or sleep? *Oh dear*...did I mix those up? They look so similar."

She shrugged and pressed a little hard for good measure. The elf turned to Asher.

"She's crazy, please don't let her—"

"She won't hurt you if you tell us what we want to know," Asher replied.

The rebel told them everything he knew. Evangeline believed him when he said he knew nothing else. His knowledge only extended as far as capturing and subduing the leaders and that they had a plan to take over the kingdoms but wasn't privy to that knowledge.

"I told you what you want. I'll sit here until it's over, just don't hurt me," he begged.

Evangeline continued to draw.

Asher got down on his level, holding his hands to the table so he couldn't try to escape.

"You've been very helpful."

Evangeline pricked his skin with the tip of the quill pen and his eyes grew wide.

"Death will suit you," she murmured as panic rose in

his face, flushing him a deep red while simultaneously making him pale. The elf's eyes fluttered as the drug overtook him.

He slumped over and Asher caught the unconscious man.

"Poisons, huh?" He smirked.

"I got bored—you can only read histories so many times," Evangeline protested.

"So you made substances that could kill a man? Does Santa know about this?"

"No, I only made the one to knock him out, the rest is just normal ink."

"You were a little too convincing of that..."

"We have more important things to be spending our time on than debating the morality and ethics of this conversation, don't we?" she questioned. "Or do we really need to have this discussion right now? Because one of us is fully studied on philosophy and ethics."

Asher propped the elf up and went to the door to summon his friends. One followed him back, helping to secure the rebel to the chair so he couldn't escape as Evangeline hid her vial so it couldn't be used against them. They left the guard in charge.

Deciding they didn't have time to go to Santa's office to monitor things, they opted to go straight to the cells to help with the rescue.

The hallway was quiet as they quickly rushed toward

the staircase to the lower level of the palace. They stayed on the carpet as much as possible to conceal the sound of their footsteps.

"You were impressive in there. It was almost captivating to watch you work," Asher broke the silence.

"*Almost*?" Evangeline replied, glancing at him. It was her finest work.

"I'm sorry you had to paint inside the lines all these years though...sounds like you could have done some extraordinary things had you been given a little freedom."

"Freedom is overrated. Security is far more important."

"I thought *knowledge* was your most important thing."

"It's one of them," she replied, hurrying to keep up. "How are we going to get to Mother Nature?"

"We need to find Ridge, Cillian, and the girls—they're likely with them now trying to free them. I'll keep you safe, we just need to get you to Mother Nature."

He turned to her, offering her something. "Take this."

Asher placed a knife in her hand. Slowing his run just enough to make sure he didn't hurt her in the transfer. She pocketed it. "Hopefully you won't need to use it with me by your side, but just in case something happens to me, you know how to use that, right?"

"Libi saw to it that we were all trained in weaponry." Cupid's daughter, though incredibly sweet, was highly skilled and ensured the other daughters were too.

Once they reached the stairs, they slowed. Asher guided their every move, checking to ensure the halls were clear before he allowed her to step out. She would have liked to have moved faster, but if the rebels had found the others, Evangeline and Asher might be the last line of defense—they needed to be cautious.

The sound of clashing swords and yelling filtered through the hallways, guiding them in the right direction. Asher sped up slightly.

He paused at the door and the two carefully peeked inside. There they found a war raging as rebels struggled to keep control of the leaders. Tempest, Ridge, Cillian, and Ciara fought. Once Santa was freed, the climate of the room changed, the fight picking up speed.

"I'll protect you. Don't worry about anything other than getting to Mother Nature and freeing her." Asher nodded to her. "It's you and me. Don't worry about anything else in there."

She nodded taking a deep breath.

CHAPTER 4

The room was chaos as Asher and Evangeline rushed in. The Winter Guard immediately threw himself into battle as Evangeline's eyes grew wide with concern.

Her sight crawled through every inch of the room searching for Mother Nature—she had to find her.

"Get down!" Tempest shouted to someone nearby. Ciara turned, dropping to the ground just in time to avoid a knife flying at her. Evangeline gasped, remaindering herself to pay attention as she picked her way through the crowd.

"Awfully sure of yourself, aren't you?" Ciara shouted back at Tempest playfully. If she hadn't ducked, she would have a knife in her back.

Tempest mumbled something back, but Evangeline couldn't hear. Knowing her friend, it was likely a sarcastic yet witty remark.

Evangeline moved through the crowd, careful to avoid

becoming entangled in the battle. Her finger glanced over the knife tucked into her pocket—she would try not to use it, but Libi had prepared her just in case.

The fighting grew louder as she ducked around people locked into a fight for their lives. Asher yelled something to her, motioning her forward.

She rushed to his side.

"I'll block for you, go!"

He turned, rushing forward as she placed a hand on his shoulder to assure him that she was by his side. Heat seared through her as her palm came into contact with his shoulder—she was walking a very dangerous line and she knew once this was all over, she was going to be in trouble.

Asher reached back, pushing her. His hand caught the side of her hip, knocking her off balance. Evangeline tumbled to the ground, falling hard on her tailbone. She rolled, ready to jump back up, but Asher's hand whipped through the air, motioning for her to stay down. Ducking, she narrowly missed being accidentally hit in the face.

Looking up from the ground, Evangeline watched as Asher collided with a rebel elf. He grunted as his sword clashed into the elf's, nearly forcing him to take a step back.

His uniform looked striking as he moved. Evangeline drew in a breath as she lifted up onto her elbows to take better stock of the room—she could barely look away from Asher and the elf.

A second elf approached, this time forcing her to roll enough to kick out at him. Her foot slammed into his ankle and the elf toppled into her, cursing.

He was heavy on top of her, pinning her to the ground as they both fumbled to untangle themselves. Her hair blocked her sight. She spit it out of her mouth as it nearly choked her, tickling the back of her throat where she accidentally swallowed part of it in her struggle.

Suddenly, the elf was lifted off of her, relieving the pressure against her chest. Asher hoisted the elf as if he weighed nothing and threw him several feet away. The elf toppled over himself, spinning on the floor as he rolled away like a doll.

Asher leaned down, offering his hand. "*Princess*."

"I hate it when you—"

"Yeah, well get used to it." He smirked.

Whipping an elbow back, he slammed it into the face of an oncoming rebel. The elf fell.

"Wow. You're really good at this." Evangeline gaped at him.

"Literally my job," he reminded her playfully. "Speaking of...you have a job too...better get on that."

She turned, hurrying to where Asher nodded—Mother Nature must be over there. She found her in the crowd and ran toward her, Asher continuing to block for her.

"Ridge!" Tempest's shriek nearly stopped Evangeline in her tracks.

In the far corner, a group of elves had Ridge cornered. One stepped forward dangerously, massive weapon in his grasp. Evangeline couldn't stop though.

"Give up or he dies," the elf shouted.

Asher jumped in front of Evangeline, whipping his sword toward the elf attempting to stop her.

"Go," he commanded.

Evangeline rushed to Mother Nature. Pulling out the knife, she started to free her.

"Mother Nature," she mumbled, hurrying to get her words out, "the drug they gave you—it started to fade the moment they gave it to you. Your powers are stronger than the others but they knew you'd stay quiet because you assumed it would grasp onto you like it did to the others."

"And you know this how, child?" Mother Nature watched her carefully.

"Father Time and Darkness are behind this," she explained. "We found one of the elves working for them and were able to break him in the interrogation. You're the only one that can stop them."

"You say it started to fade immediately?" With her hands freed, she massaged her wrists.

"Yes, that's why they were so adamant about showing you the others couldn't overcome it—because they didn't want you to even try. They used your rationale against you."

"I see." She stood. Her long hair moved around her waist. Her motions were slow and precise. "Well, then I suppose it's time to do something about this, isn't it?"

"Viv has set out to stop her father," Evangeline informed her, tugging at the bow on her sleeve. "Jubilee Claus is protecting the palace from further invasion, but you need to save Ridge."

"The boy in the corner?" Mother Nature asked, stepping forward. "I see."

"They're not going to do that," Ridge challenged the elf loudly from the corner. "They're smarter than that."

"We really are," Tempest agreed. Evangeline silently wished her friend the strength to take down the rebel and save Ridge. She knew Tempest would never recover if something happened to him.

Mother Nature nearly floated across the room her movements so graceful it was like she wasn't even walking.

"Surrender now and we'll be lenient with you." Mother Nature's voice echoed above everyone else's. Her voice was commanding and certain. She barely bothered to push back her long, flowing sleeves for the fight. "This is your final chance."

"We'll never bow to you, you—" the rebel's speech was cut off.

"Very well." A pulse rippled through the room so strongly Evangeline was shocked she didn't fall over. The elves dropped to their knees, compelled to obey. "But you should be aware—even if you stopped the others, you can only hold *my* powers back for so long."

"Siding with Father Time was only your *first* mistake," Santa stepped up by Mother Nature's side, watching her work. "Misjudging Mother Nature was your *biggest* mistake."

The floor started to split open, cracking in various locations as Mother Nature raised her hands slowly. Plantlife crept out of the broken cement floor and leeched out toward the elves.

Evangeline hadn't realized Cupid was also freed, but he stood menacingly with his bow aimed at the elf who was threatening Ridge. Under his breath, Ridge muttered something to the elf, grinning. Evangeline had always had a soft spot for him and liked having him in their group. She was sad when he and Tempest had split up—though it looked like they had reunited at some point.

The elf lunged at him anyway. Ridge stepped back, using the force to slam the elf into the wall behind him. He quickly threw his weight on the elf's back, using his knee to keep him in place as he removed the weapons from his possession.

"Are you okay?" Asher's voice frightened her as he snuck up behind her and murmured softly in her ear. She whipped around ready to yell at him, but his grin convinced her to be silent.

He slowly ran a single finger up her forearm, keeping it hidden enough that no one around them noticed.

"I'm fine, are you safe?"

"A little blood never hurt anyone." He shrugged, glancing at a few injuries he had sustained during the fight. "Anything for a pretty lady."

Evangeline stared. Asher used to flirt with her all the time when they were younger, but she had rebuffed him for so long that it had turned to animosity...apparently the sparks still lingered.

Mother Nature walked up to Ciara and brushed her hand over her arm before walking off.

"Well...that's..." Cillian tried to form a sentence, surprised that Mother Nature had so casually healed Ciara's wound.

"That's Mother Nature." Tempest shrugged, grinning. "Jubilee has told me all sorts of stories about that woman.

"*I want to be like her...*" Ciara mumbled in awe. There would be a lot of things the girl would have to get used to if she was going to stick around. Evangeline smiled to herself, thankful she had grown up in this world and didn't have to learn it at her age.

"Don't we all?" Tempest replied.

"Talking about my bravery, are we?" Ridge asked, joining them.

"Or mine…" Asher said.

"You got Mother Nature her powers back, didn't you?" Ciara turned to address Evangeline—she was perceptive.

Evangeline nodded, tugging at her dress sleeve. "He talked."

"Are you okay, Ev?" Tempest asked, eyeing her warily.

"I'll be okay." The weight and gravity of the situation cascaded over her like one of the waterfalls in her kingdom. It was heavy and overwhelming even though they had succeeded in freeing the leaders.

"I know you don't like doing that—" Tempest continued.

"I said I'll be fine," Evangeline assured her gently. Tempest looked surprised that Evangeline wasn't freaking out more. The last time she had hurt someone, she had been a wreck for over a week.

Evangeline leaned back onto her heels as Asher lingered over her shoulder.

"*Ohhh*, I see," Tempest mused animatedly. "Well won't Jubilee be surprised to see *this*?"

"She doesn't need to know." Evangeline's eyes grew wide. She wasn't even sure what this was yet—she didn't want to discuss it with anyone.

"Doesn't need to know you partnered up with her palace guard as more than just an interrogation squad?

Yeah, she's going to find out. You're telling her. Tonight. Or I'm going to tell her."

Tempest turned to walk out, clearly delighted to have information to hold over her friend. Ridge rushed to her side and she slid her arm through his, clearly reunited.

Evangeline chased after her, not willing to let it go yet. Asher caught up and laced his fingers through hers. She turned to him, surprised, but allowed it—there was no hiding now that Tempest knew anyway.

She and Tempest playfully argued all the way up the stairs to the center, only Asher's hand in hers convincing Evangeline to keep the biting tone out of her voice. He might be good for her after all.

LIBI'S SISTERS were giving directions in the center when they arrived, having been left in charge when she and Jubilee rushed off to help Viv—they still hadn't returned from the tower.

Ciara and Cillian were assigned to stand watch for them at the far entrance to the Winter Palace. The girl looked far too anxious over waiting for them, so it seemed like a good fit to have her be the one to escort them back.

"You're with me," Asher announced, grabbing Evangeline's wrist and pulling her away as he reappeared from checking in with the other guards. Tempest tossed her a look, but she ignored it. "We're checking the passageways."

He took her back to the secret hallway they had come through to find the center. Carefully, he checked to see no one was watching. Opening the door, he motioned her in.

Once inside, she was pushed back against the wall. Asher pinned her quietly, looming over her. Her hands moved to his upper arms, bracing herself as she attempted not to grin at him.

"For you," he said, opening his hand. He unveiled red flower petals.

"What is—"

"For your hair," he replied, reaching up to tuck them behind her ear like a fully-formed flower. "I liked them there."

Evangeline blushed.

"You've spent so many years pushing me away, Evangeline, but everyone *but you* knew that we were always meant to be." His voice was soft as he murmured. "I know you wanted me to leave you alone, but I couldn't because I knew it was always going to be you."

"But you didn't like me—"

"No, I was angry that you didn't see it. You wanted space and I gave it to you. That's why I threw myself into palace life—if you weren't going to be with me, I didn't want anyone, Evangeline." He moved his fingers down her hair, settling them on her neck and shoulder. "Why do you think Libi and Jubilee were always trying to push us together? They knew."

Thinking back, Evangeline saw it. As a Daughter of Love, Libi was forbidden from telling anyone who their match was, but that didn't stop her from arranging things to happen. Jubilee couldn't have known for sure, but if she picked up on what Libi was doing—as she always did—then the two of them would have worked on it together.

"Have I proven myself to you yet, Evangeline?" Asher leaned in.

Watching him, she realized how opposite they were. The way they conducted themselves, the way they engaged with people, even the way they looked and carried themselves. They complimented each other, filling out the areas the other was missing. He calmed her and she grounded him.

"Perhaps you *are* more interesting than a book, Asher."

He grinned. "You said my name. You haven't done that since we were young."

Instead of answering, she moved forward, kissing him. He immediately responded, moving his hand to her hip to pull her closer. His lips moved rapidly, drinking her in.

Evangeline's hands wove through his hair, tugging at

the strands of blond silk that shone in the dim light of the hallway. He laughed under his breath and she pulled him closer, wrapping her arm around the back of his neck.

"Making up for lost time?" He smirked at her.

Her face dropped, no longer elated. She longed to be touched by him but not if he was going to be critical. His grin disarmed her—he wasn't criticizing her; he was challenging her.

"You have a lot of work to do to catch up, *princess*. Better get to it."

She smiled, eyes pulling back wide. "Careful," she baited him. "You know how good I am at holding out on things."

"Oh *no no no*, I know your secret now. You can't fool me anymore."

He leaned down to kiss her again, fingers brushing by the petals in her hair. His touch was like fire as he lifted her against the wall, wrapping her legs around his waist. He stretched one of her arms up above her head, entwining her fingers with his.

Using her other hand, she quietly dragged the tips of her fingers against his cheek, surprising him for only a moment before he pulled back from their kiss.

"Yes, we're definitely going to make up for lost time," he assured her.

"But first, the halls?" She sighed.

"But first the halls."

She slid down the wall and allowed him to guide her through the passages, her arms wrapped around his, holding him close to her. Now that she had him, prying her off would be a task...not even Tempest's gaze could force her away.

EVANGELINE NEARLY REGRETTED NOT SPENDING MORE time in the Easter room as she and her friends danced wildly in the Christmas room—there were no falling flower petals here. Asher still stared at the two remaining petals that had managed to stay in Evangeline's hair through the dancing.

The lights flashed, making everything appear a bit more magical. The pine trees were a bit overwhelming, but it worked with the loud music raging in the room as everyone jumped into the air to the beat.

She pulled Asher closer as they danced together. She refused to look at her friends, knowing they'd be on her case about changing her mind so quickly. Libi's knowing smile would be enough to melt Evangeline into the floor so it was better not to give them the opportunity to speak about it until tomorrow.

It was enough to be dancing with her friends and Asher. Everything else could be handled tomorrow.

Tonight was just for them—to celebrate, to regroup, to recharge.

The music crashed wildly around them. Asher watched her intently, smiling softly each time she caught his gaze. This was all new to her and they'd take their time figuring out their new connection, but the spark radiated between them just as it had in the library earlier that night.

"We'll find Darkness, Viv," Tempest announced, interrupting them. "Promise. He won't get away with this."

"I know," Viv said, wrapping her arms around her fae prince—Eliad—as she nearly crashed into Jubilee. Libi smiled at her, assuring her she'd made the right choice about the dark fae prince, then turned to Evangeline to do the same. Heat crept into her dark cheeks.

Though Darkness was still out there plotting to take over, Evangeline and the girls felt ready to take him on. The leaders were freed and knew what was coming. New leadership had taken its place with Viv stepping into her new role and Prince Adaire taking on greater responsibilities. Even Evangeline had been given a new role and would be assuming new duties later that week to help win the battle against the evil forces of Darkness.

It would take time, but they would win. She was sure of it—she'd read enough history books to be able to identify the winners before the outcome had become clear to the rest.

Her friends started to slip off—for once she wouldn't be left to her own devices—she had someone to sneak off with too.

She glanced at Asher in his slightly marred uniform. He still looked incredible despite the battle wounds and marks. She had definitely picked a man that would fit well with her group of friends and their stunning men.

"Shall we?" Asher asked, offering his hand to her. "I believe there's a hallway calling our names."

Perhaps making her heart pound in secret hallways really *was* her idea of a good time.

More From The Holiday Court

Saving North (Christmas)
Reviving Time (New Years)
Targeting Bliss (Valentine's Day)
Pressing Luck (St Patrick's Day)
Hiding Destiny (Easter)
Tricking Fate (Halloween)

SAVING NORTH

Can Santa's Daughter And An Elven Prince Save The Pole?

JUBILEE HAS BEEN FORBIDDEN to interact with the refugee elven prince, Adaire, outside of work-related duties, but when Darkness attacks the Pole during the annual Holiday Court Celebration, she rushes to her secret boyfriend's aid to help stop the rebel band comprised of his former subjects.

WHEN THEY DISCOVER Darkness has enlisted Father Time to help prevent the New Year from happening, they must work with the daughters of the Court leaders to save the partygoers, free the leaders, and survive Father Time's evil plan to destroy the future for everyone.

THIS SIX-BOOK short story series features a new holiday in each installment, a powerful leading lady and her stunningly swoony man, and an epic universal party that can't possibly end at midnight.

REVIVING TIME

Can Father Time's Daughter And A Fae Prince Stop The Destruction Of The Future?

PARTY GIRL VIV knows her time is running out to live a life without the overwhelming responsibility of overseeing all of Time when her father's reign ends, so running into a handsome Fae prince at the Holiday Court Celebration is the perfect excuse to forget her future and focus on her present—Eliad—until an explosion shatters her hopes of a break.

. . .

WHEN SHE DISCOVERS Father Time has sided with Darkness to prevent the New Year from happening, Viv must work against her father to stop the destruction of time, save the partygoers, and free the leaders, even at a deadly risk to herself with the fae prince and the daughters of the Court leaders at her side.

THIS SIX-BOOK short story series features a new holiday in each installment, a powerful leading lady and her stunningly swoony man, and an epic universal party that can't possibly end at midnight.

TARGETING BLISS

Can Cupid's Daughter And A Fae Boy Rescue The Holiday Court?

As the eldest Daughter of Love, Libi and her best friend, Orion, spend their time setting up their friends whenever possible—including during the Holiday Court's annual celebration—but her self-appointed responsibility to make everyone happy gets replaced by the need to survive when the event is disrupted by rebels on a mission to destroy.

. . .

Libi's bliss quickly turns into horror when they discover Father Time is working with Darkness to destroy the future and control the Court with a mind-subduing drug that will allow them to prevent time from moving forward, and she and Orion must work quickly with the daughters of the Court leaders to save the partygoers, free the leaders, and survive the evil plot to overthrow everything they know.

This six-book short story series features a new holiday in each installment, a powerful leading lady and her stunningly swoony man, and an epic universal party that can't possibly end at midnight.

PRESSING LUCK

Can A Leprechaun's Adopted Daughter And A Shoe Maker's Son Distract The Elven Army?

CIARA HAS ALWAYS BEEN uncertain about her place in life, but when she and her boyfriend, Cillian, witness the rebels in the Holiday Court halls, she's certain she's going to have to take on some of her boyfriend's bravery to help save the others during the attack as she steps into her new role with the group.

NO LONGER AN OUTSIDER, Ciara is privy to dangerous new information about Darkness enlisting Father Time to help prevent the New Year from happening, and the rebel she helped capture could be the key. They must work with the daughters of the Court leaders to save the party-goers, free the leaders, and stop Father Time from destroying Time.

THIS SIX-BOOK short story series features a new holiday in each installment, a powerful leading lady and her stunningly swoony man, and an epic universal party that can't possibly end at midnight.

TRICKING FATE

Can A Costume Maker's Daughter And A Candymaker's Son Free the Court Leaders?

Tempest loves the lights and glamour of the Holiday Court celebration—especially since she can show off her talents in front of the Court members and her ex-boyfriend, Ridge. When she catches word of a rebel invasion, her investigation is cut short by a rippling explosion across the Winter Palace.

The daughters of the Court leaders are forced to work against Darkness' new recruit, Father Time, to save the partygoers, free the leaders, and survive the plot to stop the forwarding of Time and destroy the Holiday Court.

THIS SIX-BOOK short story series features a new holiday in each installment, a powerful leading lady and her stunningly swoony man, and an epic universal party that can't possibly end at midnight.

ACKNOWLEDGMENTS

I knew I was going to like Asher...but I didn't think I'd like Evangeline as much as I ended up liking her! I had so much fun diving into their story this morning (yes, I wrote this all in one morning!) I hope you had as much fun with this enemies-to-lovers as I did.

Special thanks to Jess for her unending support with everything I do. I'd be 100% lost without you, my lovely friend!

Thanks to the fabulous Danielle as well—your help is invaluable!

We've got one more book to go in this series and I can't wait to wrap it up—I have big things in store!

For more on Evangeline and Asher (and the other couples) be sure to hit up my website for behind the scenes!

Stay inspired!

-K.M. Robinson

WORLD PORTALS

Ready to learn exclusive facts about the Holiday Court and other K.M. Robinson Series?

World Portals are now available on www.
kmrobinsonbooks.com

Learn behind the scenes facts, watch videos, play games, check out our book filters, find out where to get bonus scenes, view fan art, and get access to other secrets we've hidden away inside the World Portals on the website.

The World Portals are constantly changing and information is being taken away and added all the time, so check back frequently for new content!

ABOUT THE AUTHOR

K.M. Robinson is a storyteller who creates new worlds both in her writing and in her fine arts conceptual photography. She is a marketing, branding and social media strategy educator who is recognized at first sight by her very long hair. She is a creative who focuses on photography, videography, couture dress making, and writing to express the stories she needs to tell. She almost always has a camera within reach. Visit her at her website: www.kmrobinsonbooks.com

CONNECT ON SOCIAL MEDIA

facebook.com/kmrobinsonbooks

instagram.com/kmrobinsonbooks

twitter.com/kmrobinsonbooks

youtube.com/kmrobinsonbooks

tiktok.com/@kmrobinsonbooks

Get free books and excerpts of other K.M. Robinson books at newsletter.kmrobinsonbooks.com

ALSO BY K.M. ROBINSON

The Golden Trilogy

Book One: Golden

Forged: A Golden Novella

Book Two: Locked

Book Three: Edge

The Complete Series Boxset/Omnibus with Tempered: an exclusive bonus novella

The Jaded Duology

Book One: Jaded

Book Two: Risen

The Complete Series Boxset/Omnibus with exclusive epilogue

The Siren Wars Saga

Book One: The Siren Wars

Book Two: Darker Depths

Book Three: Beyond The Shores

Origins of the Siren Wars: Prequel Novella

Book Four: Forbidden Waters (coming soon)

The Legends Chronicles

Along Came A Spider: A Prequel Novelette

And They'll Come Home: A Prequel Novelette

The Archives of Jack Frost Series

The Conspiracy of Jack Frost

The Redemption of Jack Frost (coming soon)

Stealing Steam Series

Book One: Lions and Lamps

Book Two: Pistons and Prisoners

Book Three: Railcars and Rulers

Top Hats and Telegraphs: A Prequel Novella

The Complete Series Boxset/Omnibus with Vambraces and Victories: an exclusive bonus novella

Virtually Sleeping Beauty: A Novella Retelling

The Goose Girl and The Artificial: A Novella Retelling

The Sinking: A Little Mermaid Novella Retelling

Cindrill: A Cinderella Assassin Novella Retelling

Sugarcoated: A Hansel and Gretel's Witch Novella Retelling

Blood Is Silent: A Red Riding Hood Circus Aerialist Retelling

Mulan Dragon Shifter

JADED: BOOK ONE OF THE JADED DUOLOGY

Her father failed in his mission to take control from the Commander, a defeat that has cost Jade her life. She will die as punishment. Now she belongs to the Commander's son—as his wife. Knowing his intent is to quietly kill her in revenge, Jade's every move is calculated to survive—until she learns her death ensures the safety of her father and her entire town.

Roan doesn't want to kill Jade, but once his family isolates her from her father and community, his only choice is to go through with the plan. Jade doesn't make it easy as she tries to sway him into falling for her. Each misstep makes him question his cause. Each moment makes every decision harder, but the Commander won't allow him to fail.

One chooses life. One chooses death. In the midst of the chaos, only one will succeed.

GOLDEN: BOOK ONE OF THE GOLDEN TRILOGY

Goldilocks wasn't naive. She was sent on a mission and Dov Baer is her new target.

When Auluria tricks the Baers into letting her into their home, they have no idea she's actually been sent by the enemy to destroy them. Intent on gathering information for her cousin to hand over to the Society seeking to destroy all of the rebel factions—including her own—she's willing to sacrifice Dov Baer to save her people... until she realizes her cousin lied to her.

Now that she's seen who Dov truly is, she has to decide between staying loyal to her only remaining family or protecting the man she's falling for. If her allegiances are discovered, either side could destroy her—assuming the Society doesn't get her first

Available now!

Learn more about The Golden Trilogy at goldeninfo.
kmrobinsonbooks.com

THE SIREN WARS: BOOK ONE OF THE SIREN WARS SAGA

War has hovered around the kingdom of Scylla for generations ever since the original sirens left the mer collection generations ago after nearly drowning the human prince. Over the years, select mermaids from the royal bloodline have been trained as spies to work for the reigning kings and queens, keeping the collection safe from sirens and humans.

Celena and her partner, Merrick, work covertly for the royals—not even her twin brother knows. When they discover the sirens have broken through the barriers the mer set up to keep the sirens out, Celena and her friends must race to the old kingdom of Metten to stop them from starting a war within their borders.

When she's dragged to the surface, Celena realizes that the war above the waters is as deadly as the one below the waves—and sacrificing herself may be the only way to protect her family.

The Siren Wars have only just begun.

Available now!

Learn more about The Siren Wars Saga at sirenwarsinfo.

kmrobinsonbooks.com

LIONS AND LAMPS: BOOK ONE OF THE STEALING STEAM SERIES

All wishes require sacrifice...*are you willing to pay the price*?

Cyra spent the last seven years being trained to steal an airship in a brutal competition that leaves the victor with millions. Last year, she won.

Aladdin spent the past year fighting to get enough money to take his mother away from Horallen after his father was murdered. Now, his evil uncle Kacper wants to force him into the competition and straight to his death inside the Collection Cave.

When Aladdin discovers a genie said to have been banished a century ago, the competition becomes even deadlier, and he knows he can't trust the girl who snuck into the competition this year...but Cyra might not survive his ruthlessness either in a game where only the lion's heart can win.

All wishes require sacrifice, and someone is going to pay the price for the Stourbridge.

Available now!

Learn more about The Stealing Steam Series at

lionsandlampsinfo.kmrobinsonbooks.com

ALONG CAME A SPIDER: THE FIRST PREQUEL NOVELETTE TO THE LEGENDS CHRONICLES

Little Hacker Muffet
sat on her tuffet
destroying her cords and Way.
Along came a hacker named Spider,
who sat down beside her
and frightened his opponent away.

When Fet, one of the most skilled hackers in the Legends, discovers her best friend and leader of her group has been abducted and held for ransom, she must escape unnoticed and find Peep before it's too late.

. . .

WHEN SPIDER, a new recruit training to join her hacker ring, slips out with her and claims to have a plan to save her friend, Fet is forced to bring him along. As she discovers he's not who he claims to be, she faces grave danger and learns just how deadly a spider bite can be.

VIRTUALLY SLEEPING BEAUTY

To wake her up, he has to enter the game and help her beat it...

SURELY THE CLASS president wouldn't illegally over-juice to stay in the virtual reality game citizens are allowed to play for four hours a day, but when Royce's aunt calls in a panic because her goddaughter hasn't left the game yet, his only option is to go inside the game and drag the girl out.

THE GOLDEN KNIGHT quickly discovers the princess' absence in the real world isn't of her own doing—*she's trapped inside the game by unknown forces*—and if she can't escape soon, she could die for real outside of the game. He's even more shocked to discover that Rora outranks him inside of the game, which means she'll have to fight to *protect herself* from the evils locking her inside a dangerous world.

CAN Rora and Royce work together to outsmart a vicious queen and evil magician, and defeat digital dragons, or will Rora slowly fade away until there's nothing left but an empty shell and the game ranking she will leave behind?

Now available!

Learn more about Virtually Sleeping Beauty at vsbinfo.kmrobinsonbooks.com

THE CONSPIRACY OF JACK FROST

No one inside the snow globe knows that Morozoko Industries is controlling their weather, testing them to form a stronger race that can survive the fall out from the bombs being dropped in the outside world—all they know is that they must survive the harsh Winter that lasts a month and use the few days of Spring, Summer, and Fall to gather enough supplies to survive.

When the seasons start shifting, Genesis and Jack know something is going on. As their team begins to find technology that they don't have access to inside their snow globe of a world, it begins to look more and more like one of their own is working against them.

. . .

GENESIS SOON DISCOVERS MOROZOKO INDUSTRIES, but when a foreign enemy tries to destroy their weather program to make sure their destructive life-altering bombs succeed in destroying the outside world, only one person can shut down the machine that is spinning out of control and save the lives of everyone inside the bunker —Jack.

SUGARCOATED

Hansel and Gretel's witch was actually on their side...

Annika's job is to create a cake to match the candy-colored rooftops, nightly firework shows, and daily parades ending in unexpected executions for the mad king's ball, but her true mission is to sneak a thirteen-year-old assassin into the palace using her gift of illusions.

Hansel's job is to protect his little sister, Gretel, once she assassinates King Levin and ends the destruction in Candestrachen, using his power over light to rescue the young girl from the chaos her influence over life and death will create.

. . .

WHEN THE ENTIRE forest reconstructs itself under Gretel's command while trying to save herself from a king's guard, Hansel and Annika must put their feelings aside and ensure their plan holds true—even if it means one of them has to sacrifice themselves to protect the mission.

Her illusions were meant to save her....but not everyone will survive the assassination attempt.

Learn more about Sugarcoated at
sugarcoatedinfo.kmrobinsonbooks.com

THE GOOSE GIRL AND THE ARTIFICIAL

What would you do if your artificially intelligent handmaiden stole your identity?

THREATENED BY HER ARTIFICIAL, Arta, Princess Goselyn is forced to switch places and pretend she isn't human when she reaches Prince Corinth to negotiate a treaty they both need to be able to take their respective crowns one day. If she doesn't comply, her Artificial, controlled by her evil cousin, will not only kill Goselyn's mother, but Prince Corinth and his father as well.

. . .

CAN the quiet princess outsmart a machine created to be more intelligent than she is, all while surviving the other Artificials and robots working against her in the foreign palace, or will Corinth and his father find out and destroy her chance to save them all?

Learn more about The Goose Girl and The Artificial at goosegirlinfo.kmrobinsonbooks.com

THE SINKING

The sea witch wants to silence her, but not for the reason you think.

When a quirky older woman pawns a fancy seashell necklace at her mother's antique shop on the pier, Cara doesn't think much about the story the woman spins about the wearer turning into a mermaid.

ON HER WAY HOME, she accidentally drops the necklace into the ocean and is swept out to sea where she meets—a merman who volunteers to take her to his mother, the sea queen, to help her get her legs back.

. . .

CARA SOON LEARNS that it's Quay's eighteenth birthday—a day that has been a curse for his family—and is meant to be one for her too. Now she must fight to survive the sea with Quay at her side.

Fans of The Little Mermaid will love this twisted take on the beloved story.

Now available!
Learn more about The Sinking at
thesinkinginfo.kmrobinsonbooks.com

CINDRILL

Cinderella is an assassin out to murder the prince...*but he's hunting her too.*

THE NANOBOTS CINDRILL'S master gives her to use as a mask allow her to slip into the ball wearing a face that isn't hers, but when the assassination attempt goes sideways, Prince Davian doesn't understand why her face changes when he injures her, slicing her foot open around a unique pair of shoes as she runs away.

WHEN CINDRILL RUNS into the prince the next day without her nanobot mask on, he doesn't recognize her, but immediately decides her skills will be useful on his hunt for the would-be-assassin woman who nearly killed his father and his fiancée the night before.

BOTH ARE TASKED with the job of murdering the other, but things don't quite go as they had planned when Cindrill's master and Davian's fiancée interfere as the two try to decide whether or not to kill the other.

IT'S hard to recognize a woman when she uses technology to change her appearance, but Cindrill is going to use that to her full advantage as she destroys the prince. ***Will either survive?***

Now available!

Learn more about Cindrill at
cindrillinfo.kmrobinsonbooks.com

BLOOD IS SILENT

Red Riding Hood is a circus aerialist and the wolf is ready to cage her.

SIENNA HAS GROWN up working for the circus, dangling off her signature red silks every night. Her grandmother has been known to wander off to train new acts for their boss, but when Sienna tries to find her to bring her back to the show, she doesn't expect the dashing and dangerous Elijah to join her.

WHEN they finally find Grandma Ida has been transformed deep in the heart of the woods, Sienna will stop at nothing to save her—but the wolf has her right where he wants her, and she won't be able to escape his claws.

SHE WAS TOLD NOT to go into the woods alone.

Now available!

Learn more about Blood Is Silent at
bloodissilentinfo.kmrobinsonbooks.com

MULAN DRAGON SHIFTER

There are no female dragon shifters in Yan Liu...except Mulan and her family. Only the enemy province has women with scales, so when they attack the Center as Mulan is dropping off her twin brother for his assignment with the army, she's forced to play the role of a non-existent brother after she shifts and rushes into the battle to protect her real twin.

TOGETHER, they must lie to their commanding officer—Mulan's secret boyfriend—and the entire army to protect her from their wrath should they find out and consider her an enemy, but Mulan's special gift might be too great to keep her secret hidden for long. She may be the only one that can save the kingdom and return the black jade blossom to the emperor.

CAN MULAN SURVIVE THE WAR, navigate two men vying for her attention, and keep her scales hidden long enough to return the province's life source to her people, or will dark, hidden forces destroy everything and cause her plans to burn hotter than her scale-melting dragon flames?

Made in the USA
Las Vegas, NV
28 January 2025

17153058R00060